This Little Tiger book belongs to:

_____

_____

_____

For Hugh
~ J C

LITTLE TIGER PRESS

An imprint of Magi Publications

1 The Coda Centre, 189 Munster Road, London SW6 6AW

www.littletigerpress.com

First published in Great Britain 2006

This edition published 2006

Printed in China

2 4 6 8 10 9 7 5 3

The Snow Angel

Christine Leeson

Jane Chapman

LITTLE TIGER PRESS
London

It was a bright, crisp morning when
a swirl of wind woke Daisy mouse
in the nest.

"Mum! Sam! Wake up," she
squeaked excitedly. "It's Christmas!
And it's been snowing!"

"Yippee!" yelled Daisy's brother
Sam, dancing round the nest.
"Happy Christmas, everyone."

"Happy Christmas, little ones," smiled Mum,
giving them each a parcel.

Daisy ripped off the wrapping. "Oooh!"
she squealed. "Berries!"

"And hazelnuts!" said Sam. "Thanks, Mum!"

Saving their presents for later, the mice rushed out to play in the snow.

"Have fun!" Mum called. "I'll find some extra bedding to make our nest cosy and later we can have a special Christmas tea."

Giggling, Daisy and Sam slipped and slid up the hillside. Below them the world sparkled under a blanket of snow but Daisy and Sam hardly noticed. High above their heads was the most beautiful thing they had ever seen. Sunshine gleamed on its wings as it soared through the sky.

"Sam, look," whispered Daisy. "It's an angel! A Christmas angel!"

But as the mice watched
breathlessly the angel
began to flutter and fall.
"Oh no!" cried Daisy,
starting forwards as it
tumbled to the ground.
"Quick!" Sam gasped.

With whiskers trembling
the mice tiptoed over
the snow.

The angel was lying silent and still. Its
feathers shone like ice, and snow crystals
glittered on its wings.

"Oh Sam!" Daisy cried. "Isn't it wonderful!"

"I don't think it looks very well," Sam
replied anxiously.

At that moment, the snowy angel spoke.

"Little mice, can you help me?" it said. "My friends and I have flown for days, from a land of ice and stars, but last night I lost them in a storm. Now I am so tired and hungry and I don't know if I will ever see them again."

"Oh dear! We need to find food," said Daisy, "but everything is frozen."

"Not everything!" said
Sam. "Come on!"
And the mice raced
off across the meadow.

The snow was getting deeper as the
mice returned, carrying their precious
parcels of berries and nuts. They lay
them in front of the lost and lonely
angel and watched as, slowly, it
began to eat.

Daisy brushed snowflakes from the angel's
wings.

"Do you think it will be all right?" she
asked as it lay its head down to sleep.

"I hope so," whispered Sam.

They waited by the angel's side until at last the snow stopped falling and sunset streaked the sky. Then the angel opened its eyes.

With a sudden rush of feathers
it spread its wings.
"Thank you, little mice," it said.
"You have been very kind. I will
never forget your help."

The mice gasped as the angel
soared up, over their heads,
shining with gold in the
evening light.

"Happy Christmas!" it called.

"Wow!" whispered Sam.

Daisy held up her paws.
"Look!" she cried. "It's
snowing again!"
White flakes whirled
around them, but as Sam
reached out and caught
one he laughed in surprise.
"Feathers!" he shouted.

Quickly the mice
gathered armfuls of
soft, white feathers
and raced back home.

"Mum!" called Daisy. "We found an angel! It gave us a present!"

Mum looked up from the straw she'd been using to line their nest.

"Goose feathers!" she sighed. "We'll feel as if we're sleeping in the clouds tonight!"

Over Christmas supper Daisy and Sam
told their mum all about their beautiful
angel. Then, happy and tired, the family
snuggled up in a warm drift of feathers.

"That was the best Christmas ever!"
Daisy whispered to Sam. "We did see
a real angel, didn't we?"

"I'm sure we did," smiled Sam.

And, as he drifted off to sleep, he saw
the feathers shining in the darkness,
glittering like stars in a frosty winter sky.

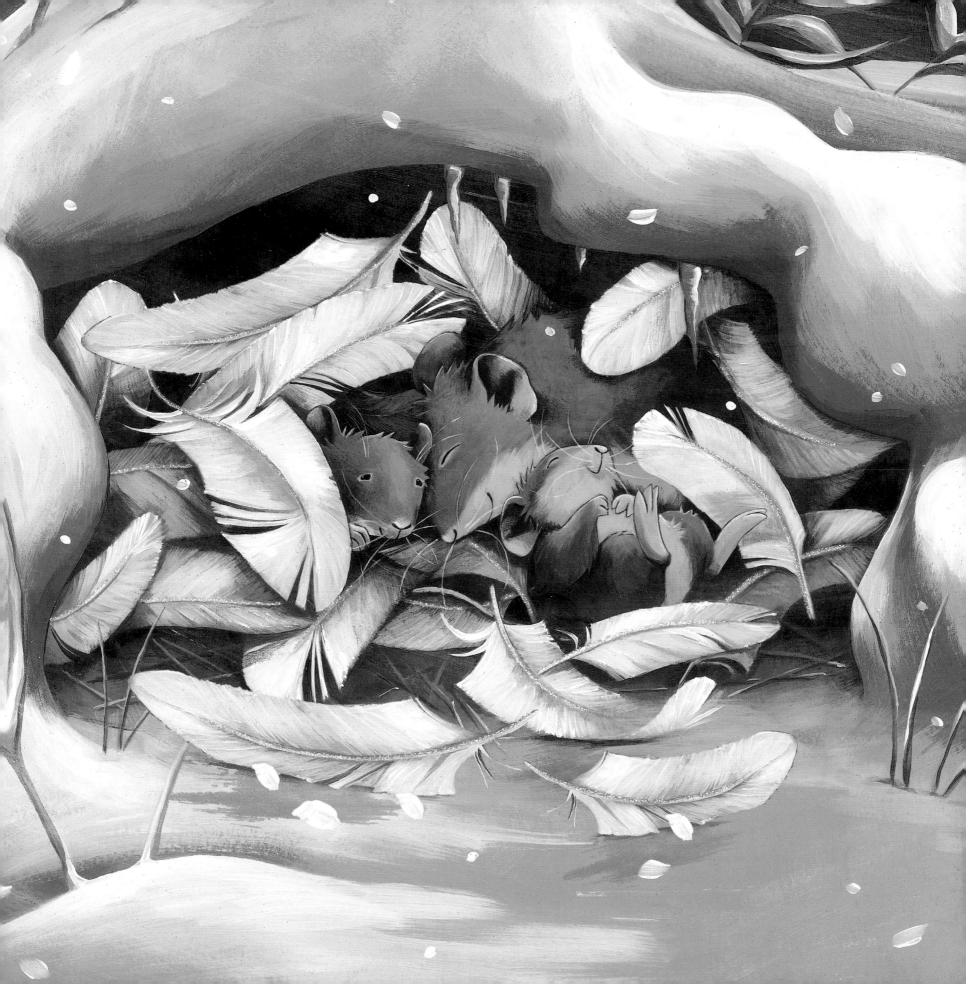

More magical books from Little Tiger Press

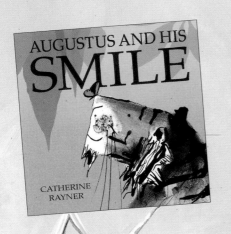

AUGUSTUS AND HIS
SMILE

CATHERINE
RAYNER

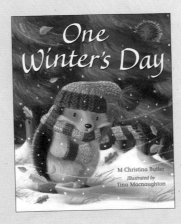

One
Winter's Day

M Christina Butler
Illustrated by
Tina Macnaughton

The Very Snowy
Christmas

Diana Hendry   Jane Chapman

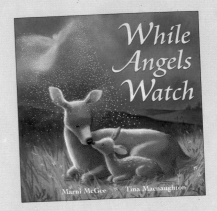

While
Angels
Watch

Marni McGee   Tina Macnaughton

Gillian Lobel
Little
Honey
Bear
and the
Smiley
Moon

Tim Warnes

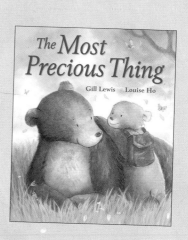

The Most
Precious Thing

Gill Lewis   Louise Ho

For information regarding any of the above titles
or for our catalogue, please contact us:
Little Tiger Press, 1 The Coda Centre,
189 Munster Road, London SW6 6AW, UK
Tel: 020 7385 6333
Fax: 020 7385 7333
E-mail: info@littletiger.co.uk
www.littletigerpress.com